There's a Gorilla on my Roof!

by Corinna O'Neill

Illustrated by Alex Crump

"How was school today Joseph?" asked Mummy.

"Fine," I replied.

"What did you do at school all day?" she enquired.

"Not much," I responded.

"Well," said Mummy. "Guess what I did today?"

Mummy came home after dropping me off at school and made herself a nice cup of tea.

Suddenly, she heard an almighty

It made her jump. She almost dropped her hot drink!

Then, it happened again:

"It sounds like someone is stomping on my roof,"
thought Mummy. Perhaps Tony, the window cleaner was fixing his ladders to the wall. She went outside to investigate.

When Mummy looked up at the roof, she had the fright of her life.

A huge brown hairy gorilla was sitting on the slates.

When the gorilla saw Mummy, it jumped. "Don't be frightened," said Mummy.

"And don't jump like that because you could fall and hurt yourself."

The gorilla looked down at Mummy with sad eyes.
"I ran away," she said, "I don't like the zoo anymore. The zookeeper wouldn't give me any broccoli."

"Well, that's a shame," said Mummy. "But you should not have run away, it could be dangerous and it's
definitely not safe up there. The important thing is, how are we going to get you down? And what is your name?"

"My name is Flo. And I didn't want to go this high," said the gorilla. "I just followed my baby up here.
She is often naughty and runs off."

Mummy was surprised. "A baby?" She took a closer look and was shocked to see a baby gorilla cradled in Flo's arm and asleep on her chest.

"Now I am really worried," said Mummy. "We must get you and your baby on the ground to safety."

Mummy wondered who she should call.

Who would have a ladder big enough to reach the top of the roof?

Who do you think?

Maybe the fire and rescue service – they have big ladders on their trucks, don't they?

No", thought Mummy, I won't call the fire rew. I know someone who can help – ony, the window cleaner."

Mummy called Tony and old him she had an mergency; he must come nmediately.

While they were waiting on Tony arriving, o asked Mummy for some broccoli.

t's my favorite food. And I need to eat efore Bam Bam wakes up," she said, ocking her baby back and forth.

ummy went inside to fetch a big chunk f roccoli from the fridge.

he flung her arm high towards the sky o throw the vegetable on to the roof. It ame tumbling down. She tried again:

, 2, 3 whoosh, up it went, and Flo caught . She quickly munched it all up.

Next thing, Mummy heard a beep. It was Tony in his van.

"What on earth is the emergency?" asked Tony.
"Look up," replied Mummy.

Tony got his long extension ladders and placed them against the wall. He slowly climbed up and reached out to Flo.

"Give me the baby first," said Tony. Flo handed over Bam Bam, who had woken up and seemed quite excited by all the fuss. He gave Bam Bam to Mummy who wrapped her in a cosy blanket. Then Tony went back up to help Flo down. Flo was very agile and was able to quickly descend the ladder without any help.

"Now we need to get you back to the zoo," said Mummy.

Luckily Tony had a big van. He helped Flo and Bam Bam into the back, and they sat on the blanket.

Just as they were about to leave, Bam Bam made a snorting noise and said "wuw uw". "She's still learning to talk," said Flo and she fed her some milk.

WINDOWS

When they got to the zoo, the zookeeper came out and threw his arms in the air.

"Hooray, thank goodness you're back Flo," he said. "We have all been worried sick. Why did you climb the fence and run away like that?"

Mummy told him about the broccoli, and the zookeeper explained that they had been unable to get enough delivered so had to serve bananas instead.

The zookeeper took Flo and baby Bam Bam back to their enclosure and they waved goodbye to Mummy.

As she made the journey home in Tony's van,
Mummy thought about the adventurous day she'd had.
She couldn't wait to tell me all about it.

Maybe I should tell her more about my day.

know parents love to hear what their
...ildren are doing at school and it's
...ways important to let them know how
...u're feeling.

Printed in Great Britain
by Amazon